The Purple Boots

by Liza Charlesworth
illustrated by Rachel Moss

ISBN: 979-8-225-02079-8

Publisher: Tara Welty
Creative Director: Tannaz Fassihi; Designer: Cynthia Ng

1 2 3 4 5 6 7 8 9 10 68 34 33 32 31 30 29 28 27 26 25

Made in Jiaxing City, China. First printing, August 2025.

SCHOLASTIC

Howdy, partner! My name is Callie Jones.
My home is a small town in the desert.
I like to ride horses and hunt for lizards.
What else do you need to know? Oh, yes!
Yesterday was my birthday. I turned ten.
How was my birthday? Spooky and fun!
Keep reading and I'll tell you all about it.

Yesterday morning, I woke up and went down the stairs. Did I see my mom or dad? Nope! But what I saw was quite shocking. Out the back window, I spotted a pair of purple cowgirl boots running across the grass. And here's the creepy thing: There was NOBODY inside of them!

What do you think happened next? Well, those boots jumped on a rock and did a funky jig. Hip, hop, hip, hop! Then they dashed up the steps to our back door and just stood there. Hmmm? Did that mean the spooky boots were a birthday gift for me?

They looked to be the right size.
But, when I swung open the door
to grab them, the purple boots
took off in a flash and ran away.
There was just one thing for a kid
like me to do: chase after them!

Race and chase, race and chase!
Yee-haw! Those boots were fast.
They ran right past the fish pond
and into our big red barn. Yikes!
What did they do next? The boots
climbed to the top of a haystack. . .

and did the chicken dance with a hen.
"Cluck, cluck!" she yelped with glee.
Then, the brown cow said, "Moo, moo!"
The gray goat said, "Bleat, bleat!"
And the pink pig said, "Oink, oink!"
The critters liked the show a whole lot!

After that, the boots ran back outside.
Race and chase, race and chase!
They dashed into the veggie garden
and zig-zagged between the peppers
and pumpkins and teeny green peas.
Then, just to mock me, they stopped
and boogied beside the scarecrow.

Closer and closer I crept. I reached out my hands to grab them. Did I succeed? Nope! Quick as a wink, the frisky boots kicked up their heels and darted away down a long, dusty path.

Race and chase, race and chase!
The boots didn't quit until they reached
the center of town, where they wrote
a note in the sand. It said, HOWDY, CALLIE!
Golly, gee! How did they know me?
To make matters even more spooky,
I did NOT see even a single person.

It was just me and those purple boots. Then—click, clack! They turned around and strolled into the Wild West Diner. Leaping lizards! What was going on? I had to know, so I trailed them inside.

Yikes! The diner was silent and pitch-black. I felt quite afraid, so I stepped with care. Then I spotted them. Where? The boots were standing on top of a wooden crate. And here is the spookiest thing: A glowing, purple ghost had them on her two feet!

What happened next? She spoke to me:
“Howdy, partner! I’m so glad you came.
I am a cowgirl ghost in fine purple boots.
But I’m only visible in complete darkness.
That is why you did not see me before.
I needed to lead you here for a reason.”

“OK,” I gulped. “Can you tell me the reason?”
“When I flip on the light, I’ll vanish from sight.
But you will understand. Got it?” she said.
“Yup. I think so,” I replied with a shiver.
Then, just as she stated, the ghost flipped
on the light and I got the shock of my life.

My mom and my dad plus everyone in my whole town screamed, “SURPRISE! HAPPY TENTH BIRTHDAY, CALLIE!” Leaping lizards! That ghost had a plan. She made me chase her purple boots—all the way to my own surprise party!

Yee-haw! I felt thankful for the cake and gifts—
but most of all, for my super spooky adventure.
As I peeked out the window, I spotted those
purple boots sprinting off into the sunset.
But now I knew they were not a bit empty.
A sweet cowgirl ghost was inside of them!